![Miss Spider's Sunny Patch Friends]

Sing It, Sister!

David Kirk

GROSSET & DUNLAP/CALLAWAY

This book is based on the TV episode "Sing It, Sister!" written by Steven Sullivan, from the animated TV series *Miss Spider's Sunny Patch Friends* on Nick Jr., a Nelvana Limited/Absolute Pictures Limited co-production in association with Callaway Arts & Entertainment, based on the Miss Spider books by David Kirk. Special thanks to the Nelvana staff, including Doug Murphy, Scott Dyer, Tracy Ewing, Pam Lehn, Tonya Lindo, Susie Grondin, Luis Lopez, Eric Pentz, and Georgina Robinson.

Cover digital art by Mark Picard.

Library of Congress Control Number: 2005017698

ISBN 0-448-43974-3   10 9 8 7 6 5 4 3 2

One day, Miss Spider's children heard Katy Katydid and the Dribbly Dell Singers practicing in the meadow.

"The Dribbly Dell Singers are the best!" Pansy exclaimed.

"You know," Squirt said, "I hear that they're holding tryouts for a new singer."

"Really? Maybe I could join them," Pansy sighed dreamily.

That evening, Pansy practiced for her big tryout. But her voice didn't sound very good— it was squeaky and screechy.

"Maybe you should practice a little bit more, Pansy," Holley suggested.

"I don't need to practice, Dad," she laughed. "I know all the words!"

"I don't think Pansy is ready," whispered Holley to Miss Spider.

"Maybe not," Miss Spider said, "but she should have the chance to follow her dream."

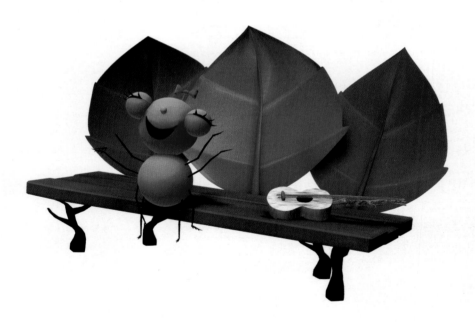

Suddenly, they heard a beautiful voice coming from outside. Holley and Miss Spider found Snowdrop singing on her swing.

"With a pretty voice like that, maybe you should try out for the Dribbly Dell Singers, too," Holley suggested.

"Oh, I could never sing in front of other bugs," said Snowdrop shyly. "I would be too embarrassed!"

At tryouts the next day, Pansy sang her heart out. But her voice was still squeaky and screechy.

"That was a real good try, darlin'," Katy began, "but I think you may need to practice just a little bit more."

Pansy shuffled off with tears in her eyes.

"My voice was all squeaky, and I forgot the words, and I can't sing at all!" Pansy cried to her mom when she came home.

"Oh, honey," soothed Miss Spider. "I'm *so* sorry."

The two looked up as Snowdrop's beautiful singing filled the room. Pansy followed the music outside.

"**W**ow!" said Pansy. "Do you think you could teach me to sing like that?"

"Sure! Singin' while you're swingin' helps you keep your rhythm!" Snowdrop sang.

Pansy joined her in perfect harmony. "Hey, I sing a lot better when I'm with you!" she smiled.

Pansy practiced with Snowdrop and decided to try out again.

A few days later, Katy had still not found the next Dribbly Dell Singer.

Miss Spider poked her head in the door of the concert hall. "Pansy would like to give it another try," she said.

But when Pansy got onstage, she was so nervous, she forgot the words!

Snowdrop tried to help her. "Like this, Pansy: Bu-bu-BUTTERFLIES," she sang sweetly.

Katy's face lit up as she heard Snowdrop's lilting voice. "Snowdrop, your voice is prettier than the breeze in the pine trees!" she exclaimed. "I do believe we've found our next Dribbly Dell Singer!"

Pansy ran off in tears. Snowdrop felt terrible.

"It's not fair, Mom," Pansy sobbed. "I should have been the new Dribbly Dell Singer!"

"Honey, Snowdrop didn't mean to hurt your feelings," Miss Spider said gently. "Singing just happens to be her special talent. Maybe you could try to be happy for her."

"I'll try," Pansy sniffled. "But it won't be easy."

Snowdrop practiced all week for the Dribbly Dell Singers concert. Finally, it was the night of the show. The entire family was getting ready to watch her perform.

Pansy came down the stairs with a big grin on her face. "I was sad at first," she said, "but now I can't wait to see Snowdrop sing in the concert!"

"That's great, sweetie!" Miss Spider exclaimed. "But where is Snowdrop?"

They found Snowdrop on her swing outside.

"Don't you want to be in the show tonight?"
Miss Spider asked.

"I'm too embarrassed!" Snowdrop said shyly.
"I don't want to sing in front of all of those
other bugs!"

"Don't worry," Pansy said as she crawled over. "If you get nervous, just look out at me and pretend we're singin' and swingin' with each other!"

The two began to hum a tune.

"You two sing so beautifully together," Miss Spider remarked. "I have an idea!"

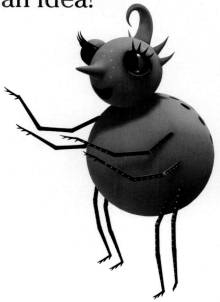

The hall was filled with bugs eager to see the concert.

"We have a last-minute surprise that's sure to double your listening pleasure," Katy announced.

Snowdrop and Pansy came onstage and sang a beautiful duet. Their glorious voices soared through the concert hall.

"**W**ow!" Squirt exclaimed. "Pansy sure sounds better than she did before."

"That's because she practiced a lot," said Holley.

"And she had a sister who was there to help her," Miss Spider added.

Pansy and Snowdrop's duet ended with a flourish, and the sisters smiled brightly as the concert hall rang with applause.